Care-Bear

Christmas Surprise

Written by Jenny McPherson
Illustrated by Jeff Harter and Warner McGee

SCHOLASTIC INC.

New York   Toronto   London   Auckland   Sydney
Mexico City   New Delhi   Hong Kong   Buenos Aires

ISBN-13: 978-0-545-00907-2
ISBN-10: 0-545-00907-3

12 1I 10 9 8 7 6 5 4 3 2 1   7 8 9 10/0

Printed in the U.S.A.

First printing, November 2007

Designed by Michael Massen

Christmas was right around the corner, and all over Care-a-lot, the Care Bears were busy pitching in to make their town as merry as could be.

Inside Funshine Bear's house, it was warm and cozy. Funshine and his friend Cheer Bear were putting up Christmas decorations. "Thanks for helping out, Cheer," said Funshine. "You made my house look truly *cheerific!*"

Meanwhile, at the Toy Shop, Oopsy Bear was helping Share Bear put up the Christmas toy display when suddenly . . .

OOPSIE!

"Don't be sad, Oopsy," said Share Bear to her friend. "We all make mistakes sometimes. I'll help you clean up this mess!"

Oopsy tried to sweep up the broken toys, but he bumped into a toy shelf. The shelf knocked over another shelf and another like a row of dominoes until . . .

Oopsy had an idea. "I'll make new toys!" he exclaimed. Making toys was hard. "I'll never be able to finish these on my own," he thought out loud. Share Bear heard Oopsy and knew just what to do. She ran straight to Funshine Bear's house.

Share Bear told Funshine and Cheer what had happened at the Toy Shop. "If we all work together, we can help Oopsy make the toys in time for Christmas," Share said.

Soon the Toy Shop buzzed with activity. Each Care Bear had a job to do, and Oopsy had a very special one — passing out yummy treats to his friends!

"I wish every Christmas could be this fun!" exclaimed Wish Bear.

The Care Bears worked hard into the night
and all through the next day.

Finally, on Christmas Eve, all of the toys were done. "Time to celebrate!" exclaimed Oopsy proudly, grabbing for a toy trumpet.

"Oopsy, no!" cried out Good Luck Bear, but it was too late. The pile of toys came tumbling down.

All the toys that the Care Bears had worked so hard to make were now broken.

"Oopsy, you've ruined Christmas!" grumbled Grumpy Bear. Oopsy was sad.

The Care Bears laughed and sang carols and played until it was time for bed. It was the merriest Christmas Eve Care-a-lot had ever seen!

The next morning, when Oopsy woke up, he had almost forgotten it was Christmas. That is, until he walked by Care Square and saw the big tree. "It's a Christmas surprise!" Oopsy called out as loud as he could.

All the Care Bears came to see the Christmas surprise. Nestled under the branches of the big tree were dozens of colorful Christmas presents!

"But we discovered that Christmas is about love and friendship and not just toys," said Cheer Bear.

"And that made all of our
Christmas wishes come true!"

Merry Christmas, everyone!